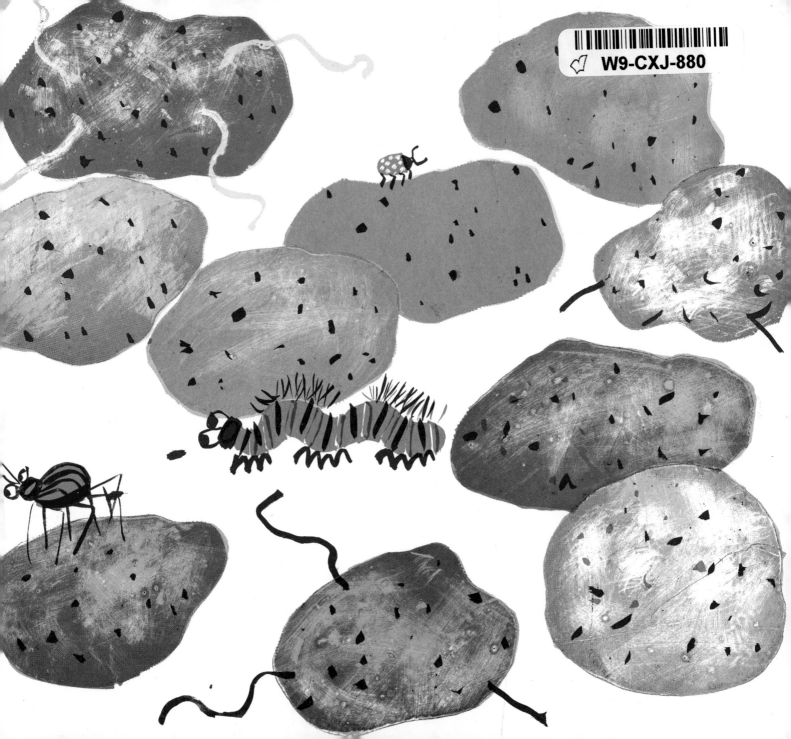

THE HUNGRY LEPRECHAUN

THE HUNGRY LEPRECHAUN

written by
MARY CALHOUN

illustrated by
ROGER DUVOISIN

WILLIAM MORROW AND COMPANY NEW YORK 1962

Once upon a time, and a very hard time it was, too,
everyone in Ireland was poor.
The Irish ground was so poor
it grew little but rocks and dandelions.
Young Patrick O'Michael O'Sullivan O'Callahan was so poor
he had only dandelion soup to eat.

Even the leprechauns were poor,
not a pot of gold amongst them.
But Patrick O'Michael O'Sullivan O'Callahan didn't know that.
He believed in leprechaun magic,
and he believed that if only he could catch a leprechaun,
he'd be rich.
He'd make the little man give him his gold.
So every day when young Patrick went out
to dig dandelions for dinner,
he watched sharply for a stray leprechaun.
Now the littlest of all little men
lived in a cave under the hill by Patrick's house.
His name was Tippery,
and he was very, *very* hungry.
One day, much as he feared to,
he came out in broad daylight looking for something to eat.

And it happened that Patrick O'Michael was nearby,
digging his dandelions.
Quick, sharp! he spied the little man.
And quick, jump! he flopped his hat over the creature.
He'd caught him!
Patrick O'Michael O'Sullivan O'Callahan
had caught himself a leprechaun!
"Give me your gold, or I'll never let you go,"
ordered Patrick, all eager and gay.
"I haven't any gold, no more than you,"
said Tippery, all miserable and hungry.
"Are dandelions good for eating?"

Then Patrick O'Michael peeked under his hat,
and he saw that he'd caught
the thinnest, the weakest, the most hungry-looking leprechaun
that ever lived.

And he was sorry for the little man.
"Dandelion soup is better than nothing at all,"
he told Tippery.
"I'll take you home and feed you some."
That he did.
Tippery's long, narrow ears perked up
when he saw his bowl of dandelion soup.
He sniffed it with his round nose.
And then he lapped it up with his pointed tongue.

But Patrick O'Michael O'Sullivan O'Callahan
still believed in leprechaun magic,
and he cried, "Whoever heard of a leprechaun
with no magic to make gold! For shame!"
Tippery's long ears drooped.
He'd used up most of his magic in the hard times.
"Come now, where do you keep your magic?" Patrick insisted.
"In your pocket? In your left shoe?"
"In my finger tips, of course," said the leprechaun.
"But I was saving my wee bit for the worst time of all."
"Oho!" Young Patrick sprang up.
"That worst time has come, my little man.
I command you to turn this pot of dandelion soup into gold!"
"I'm still hungry," Tippery complained.
"Will you make more soup if I do?"
Patrick agreed.
Now changing the soup into gold was stirring magic.
But what to stir with?

It had been so long since Tippery had made magic
that he'd almost forgotten how.
He screwed up his nose to think,
and he pulled his left ear.
"Oh me, let me see," he muttered.
Patrick danced about in a dither of eagerness.
"Aha!" said Tippery.
He blew on his fingers to warm up the magic.
Then he stirred the soup with the feather from his cap.
But the dandelion soup only spit at him.

"Maybe—" said Tippery.
He stirred the soup with a broomstraw—
and the dandelions curled up.
"Or was it—?" said Tippery.
He hung over the edge of the pot
and stirred with his long left ear.
The dandelion soup rumbled and roiled.
The dandelions disappeared.

And when the steam cleared,
Tippery had a potful of—frogs!
Little green frogs hopping about.
Tippery's ears hung down.
"I forgot how to make stirring magic," he said.
"Let's dig dandelions and make some more soup."
"No, no. Have faith.
You can do it," urged Patrick O'Michael.

He pointed to the yellow puddle of sunlight on the floor.
"Sure now, you can change that into purest gold," he said.
That was sprinkling magic.
But what to sprinkle with?
The leprechaun bit his pointed tongue,
and he pulled his right ear.
"Oh me, let me see," said Tippery.

"I wonder—" he said.

He dibbled his magic fingers in the puddle of sunlight.

Then he sprinkled it with ashes from the hearth.

The sunlight grew runny.

"It's coming, it's coming!" shouted Patrick O'Michael.

Suddenly it turned into a puddle of water.

Hop, skip, quicker than jump!

The frogs were in the puddle, splashing happily.

Tippery slunk under the table, but Patrick hauled him out.
"Try once more," he begged.
By this time Tippery had used up all of his magic
except what was in one little finger.
Besides, he was very, *very* hungry.
"Let's dig dandelions first," he said.
So Patrick and Tippery went out to the fields
and dug dandelions.

When they had a big pile,
young Patrick pointed to all the rocks in the field.
"If only you could change those rocks into gold," he said.
That was touching magic, hardest kind of all.
Tippery had to get the magic in his little finger
lined up just right and—
there was something he couldn't remember.
"Oh well," said Tippery.
He grabbed both ears and whirled around three times.
He reached his little finger out to the rock,
touched it—
and there was a golden flash!

Quick, fast, Tippery ran about the field
touching rocks with his little finger
until all its magic had run out.
Then Tippery and Patrick O'Michael looked at the rocks.
But not a glitter of gold did they see.
The rocks were still brown.
Wait, there was one thing that glittered—Tippery's finger.
Tippery's little finger had turned into gold!
Oh, the disgrace!
Tippery looked for a place to hide.
"Oh, begorra!" Patrick O'Michael wailed.
"What good is a golden finger?
I *would* catch the most forgetful leprechaun in all Ireland!"

And he gave one of the rocks a mighty whack
with his dandelion shovel.
But what was that?
The rock split open, and it was white inside.
Tippery poked it.
He smelled it with his round nose.
He licked it with his pointed tongue.
"We might try boiling it," he said.
Patrick and Tippery gathered up some of the hard, brown things
and took them home.
They put them in a pot of boiling water.

When the things had cooked,
Patrick and Tippery each took a bite,
and the things were *good!*
"They may not be gold,
but they're good to eat!" shouted Patrick O'Michael.
"Hooray!" cried the little man.
"We put them in the *pot,* and we *ate* them.
We'll call them potatoes!"
Then young Patrick and his leprechaun
had fried potatoes for breakfast,
and baked potatoes for dinner,
and potato soup for supper.
The next day they added dandelion greens to the potatoes
and had potato salad.

But they didn't eat all the potatoes.
Tippery said they must save some to plant.
Which they did.
When the new potatoes sprouted, they gave some to their neighbors,
and then those neighbors gave some to other neighbors.
Soon all Ireland had potatoes.
But to this day, only the children's children of
Patrick O'Michael O'Sullivan O'Callahan
remember that they can thank a hungry leprechaun for potatoes.

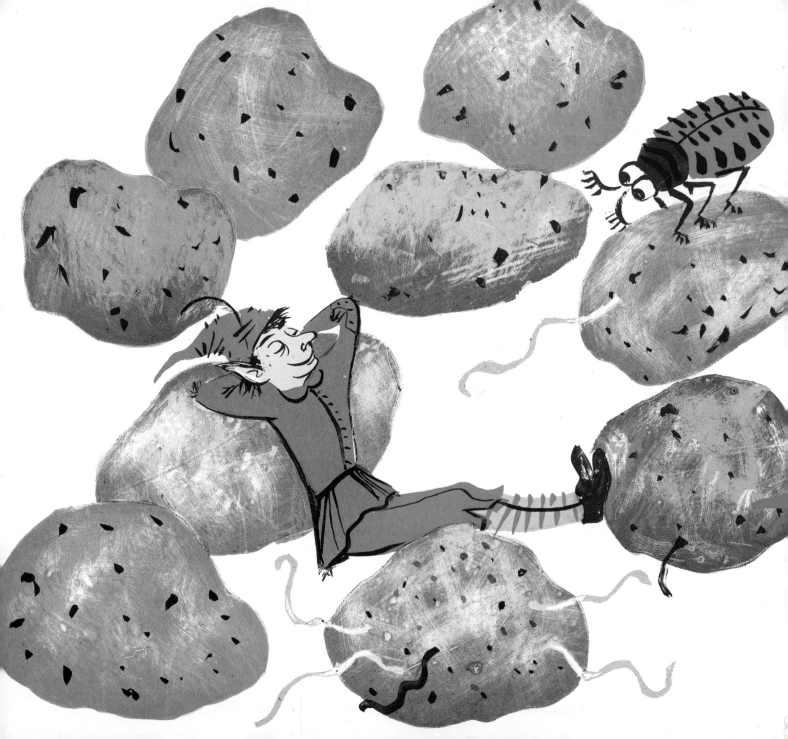